PAUL BUNYAN

A tall tale
retold and illustrated by

STEVEN KELLOGG

WILLIAM MORROW & COMPANY · NEW YORK 1984

This book is a presentation of Atlas Editions, Inc.
For more information about Atlas Editions
book clubs for children write to:
Atlas Editions, Inc., 4343 Equity Drive, Columbus, Ohio 43228.

2000 Edition

Printed in the USA

Published by arrangement with William Morrow & Company, Inc.

READING RAINBOW® is a registered trademark of GPN/WNED-TV.

Library of Congress Cataloging in Publication Data
Kellogg, Steven.   Paul Bunyan.
Summary: Recounts the life of the extraordinary lumberjack whose unusual size and strength brought him many fantastic adventures. 1. Bunyan, Paul (Legendary character)—Juvenile literature. [1. Bunyan, Paul (Legendary character) 2. Folklore—United States. 3. Tall tales] I. Title.   PZ8.1.K3Pau   1984
398.2'2'0973   [E]   83-26684   ISBN 0-688-03849-2   ISBN 0-688-03850-6 (lib. ed.)

For my heroic nephew, Steve Hoffman

Paul Bunyan was the largest, smartest, and strongest baby ever born in the state of Maine.

Even before he learned to talk, Paul showed an interest in
the family logging business. He took the lumber wagon and
wandered through the neighborhood collecting trees.

There were so many complaints about Paul's visits that his
parents anchored his cradle in the harbor.

All was well until Paul started rocking the cradle and
stirring up waves.

After his parents had paid for the damage, they decided to
move to the backwoods where life would be more peaceful.

Paul loved his new wilderness home. He soon grew into a sturdy lad who was so quick on his feet he could blow out a candle and leap into bed before the room became dark.

Every day he joined his forest friends in their sports.
He raced with the deer and wrestled with the grizzlies.

One morning Paul awoke to find the world under a blanket of blue snow. He heard a moan from inside a snowdrift, and there he found a shivering ox calf. Paul adopted him and named him Babe.

Both Paul and Babe began growing at an astonishing rate, but the ox never lost the color of the snow from which he'd been rescued.

As the years passed, the two of them proved to be extremely helpful in the family business.

At seventeen, Paul grew a fine beard, which he combed with the top of a pine tree.

By this time other settlers were beginning to crowd into the Maine woods. Paul felt an urge to move on. He said good-bye to his parents and headed west.

Paul wanted to cross the country with the best lumbering crew available. He hired Ole, a celebrated blacksmith, and two famous cooks, Sourdough Slim and Creampuff Fatty. Then he signed up legendary lumbermen like Big Tim Burr, Hardjaw Murphy, and the seven Hackett brothers.

Paul put the camp buildings on wheels so that Babe could haul them from one forest to another. As soon as he had cleared the land, pioneers moved in to set up farms and villages.

On the far slopes of the Appalachian Mountains,
several of Paul's men were ambushed by a gang of
underground ogres called Gumberoos.

Paul grabbed the camp dinner horn and blew
a thunderous note into the Gumberoos' cave,
determined to blast the meanness right out of them.

To Paul's dismay, the Gumberoos responded by snatching the entire crew. A wild, rough-and-tumble rumpus began inside the den.

When that historic tussle was over, the Gumberoos needed six weeks to untangle themselves.

They disappeared into the depths of the earth, and they've never been heard from since.

Paul's next job was to clear the heavily forested midwest.
He hired armies of extra woodsmen and built enormous
new bunkhouses. The men sailed up to bed in balloons
and parachuted down to breakfast in the morning.
Unfortunately the cooks couldn't flip flapjacks fast enough
to satisfy all the newcomers.

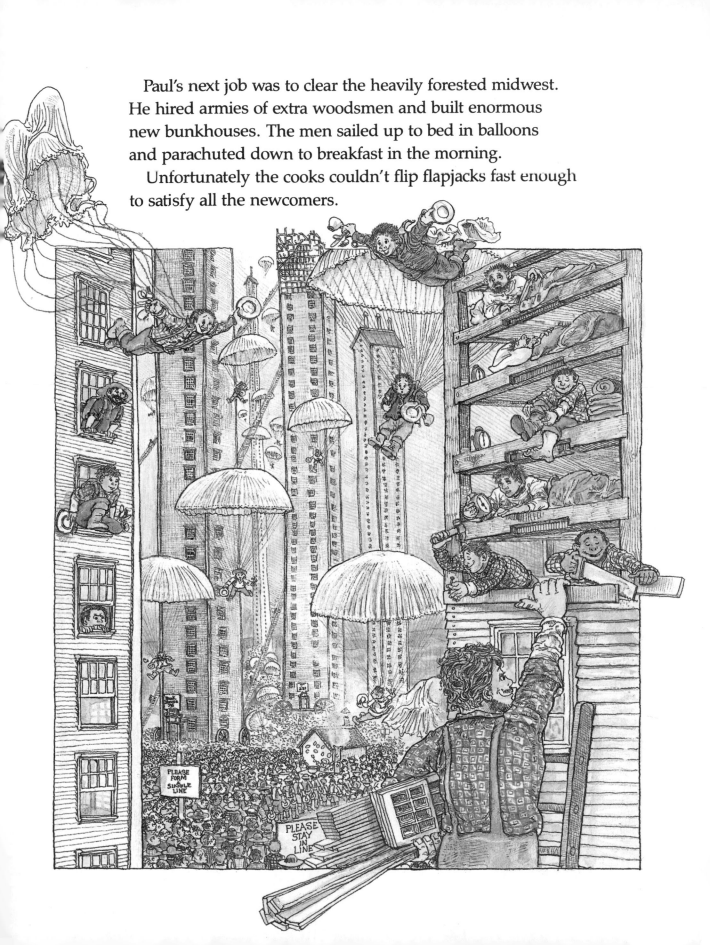

To solve the muddle, Paul built a colossal flapjack griddle. The surface was greased by kitchen helpers with slabs of bacon laced to their feet.

Everytime the hot griddle was flooded with batter,
it blasted a delicious flapjack high above the clouds.
Usually the flapjacks landed neatly beside the griddle,
but sometimes they were a bit off target.

Paul took a few days off to dig the St. Lawrence River and the Great Lakes so that barges of Vermont maple syrup could be brought to camp.

Fueled by the powerful mixture of flapjacks and syrup, the men leveled the Great Plains and shaved the slopes of the Rocky Mountains.

They probably would have sawed the peaks themselves into logs if a blizzard hadn't suddenly buried the entire mountain range.

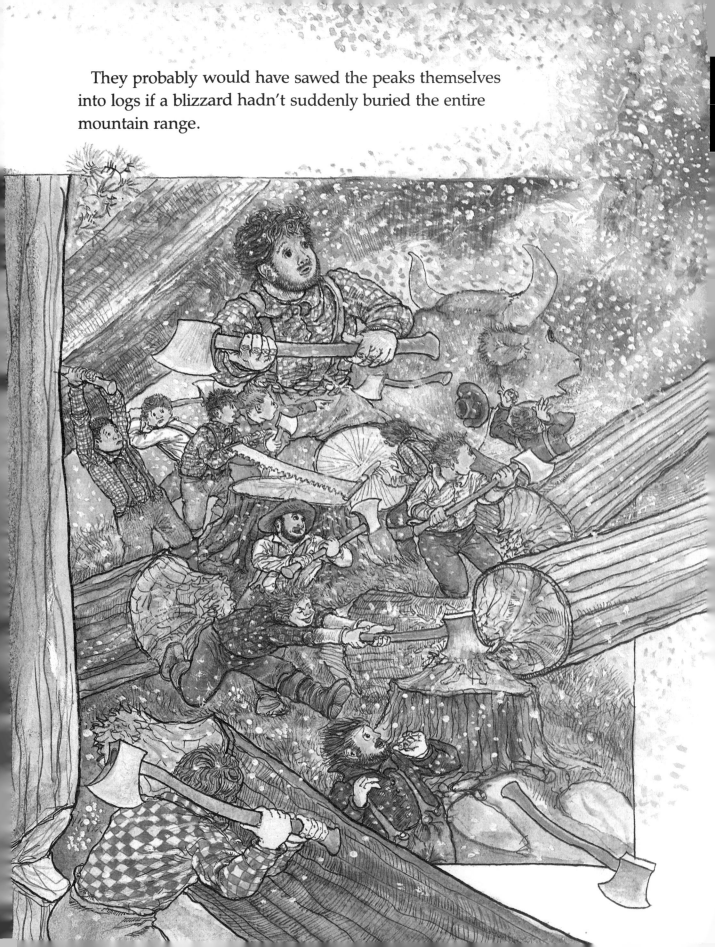

That blizzard continued for several years, snuffing out the springs, summers, and autumns. The crew burrowed into their bunkhouses and hibernated.

Babe became so depressed that Paul asked Ole to make
a pair of sunglasses for his friend.

When Babe saw the world colored green, he thought he'd
stumbled into a field of clover. He began eating the snow
with such gusto that soon the treetops reappeared.

At that point, all those pent-up springtimes simply exploded, dissolving the storm clouds and the remaining snow.

Paul and his friends invited some newly arrived settlers to join
them in a celebration of all the holidays that had been missed.

After the festival the lumberjacks continued their journey. But, as they headed southwest, the blistering sun and the giant Texas varmints proved to be more of a problem than they had expected.

Travel became so difficult that some of the men
began to speak longingly of being buried by
a blizzard or bear hugged by a Gumberoo.

While crossing Arizona the griddle curled up like a burned leaf, and the batter evaporated. Deprived of their flapjacks, the lumbermen became weak and discouraged.

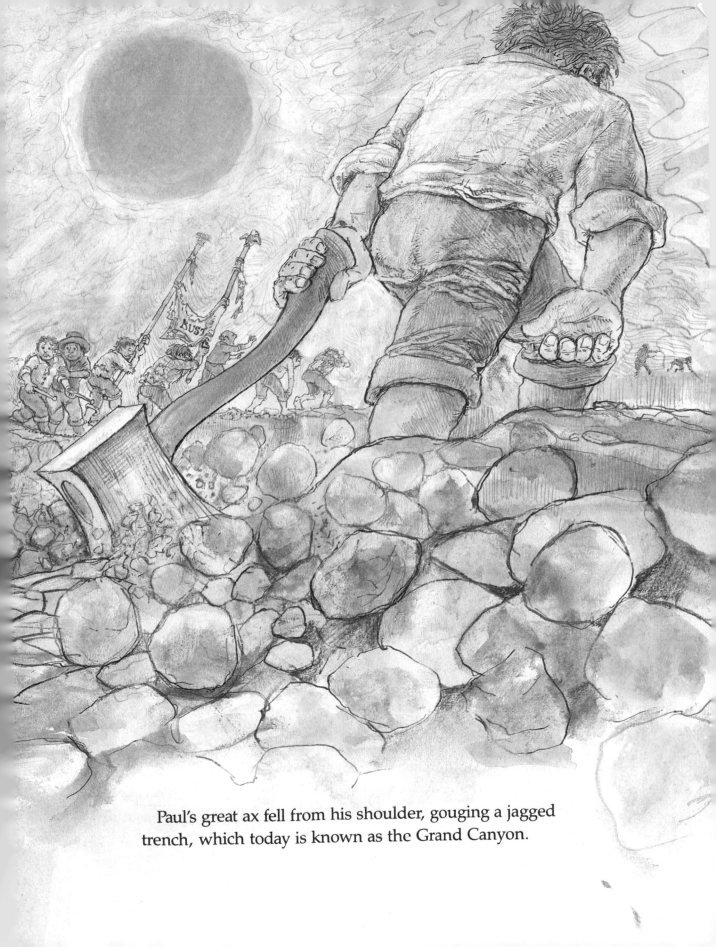

Paul's great ax fell from his shoulder, gouging a jagged trench, which today is known as the Grand Canyon.

Disaster seemed certain until Paul came up with a desperate plan. He headed east and found a family that could sell him a barn filled with corn.

Babe galloped it back across the desert.

When the flaming sunrise hit that barn it exploded, and the lumbermen awoke to find themselves in a raging blizzard of popcorn. Dizzy with joy, they pulled on their mittens and began blasting each other with popcorn balls.

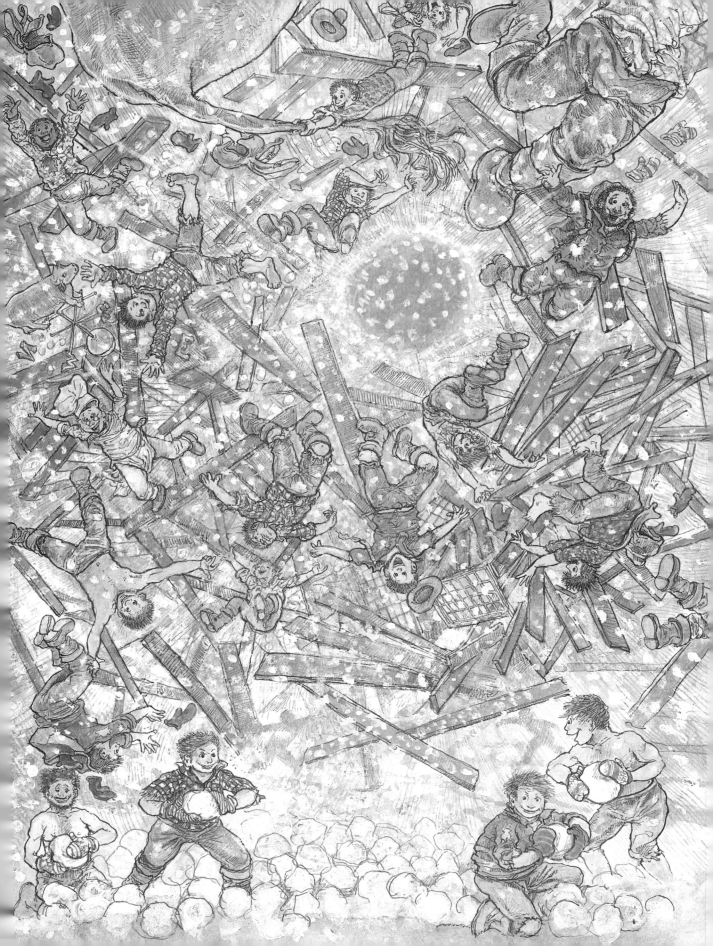

A westerly wind kept the cooling clouds of popcorn swirling around Paul and his crew until they crossed California and reached the Pacific Ocean.

After he had crossed the country, some say that Paul gave up lumbering and rambled north searching for new areas of untouched wilderness.

With the passing years, Paul has been seen less and less frequently. However, along with his unusual size and strength, he seems to possess an extraordinary longevity. Sometimes his great bursts of laughter can be heard rumbling like distant thunder across the wild Alaskan mountain ranges where he and Babe still roam.

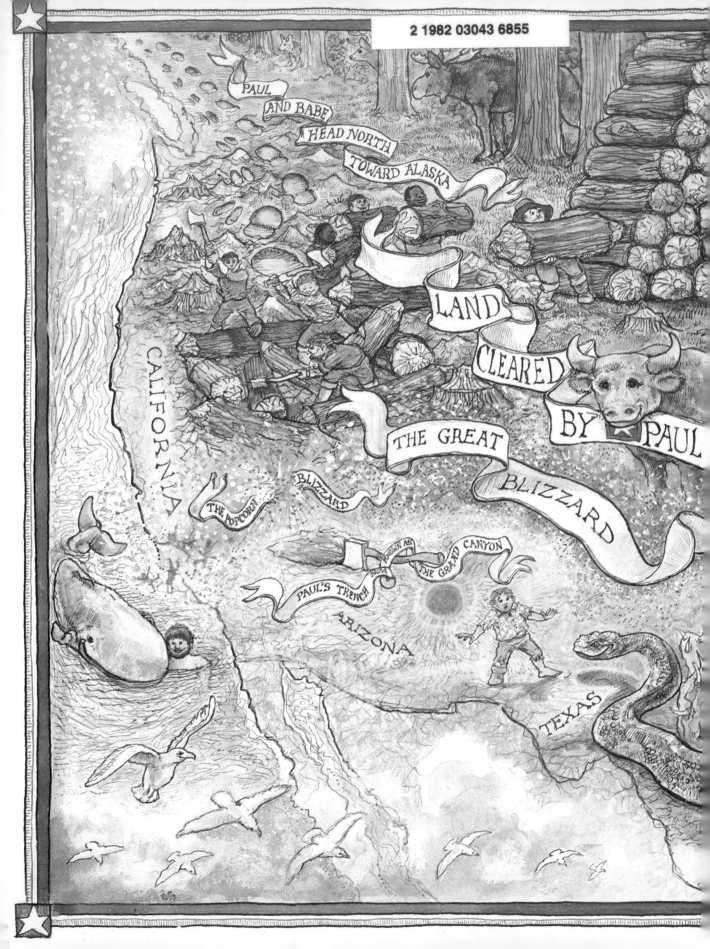